# TOLLY

J PATRICK LEMARR

WRITE CROWD PUBLISHING

*For Dad*

# CONTENTS

# TOLLY

My name is Nevaeh Wheaton, and I have been an investigative journalist for 17 years. In that time, I've established a reputation as someone who relentlessly seeks the truth. This ferocity has earned me several prestigious awards and opportunities most young journalists would kill for. It never mattered to me. I wasn't hunting fame or fortune. I never cared about being a network anchor or sitting on a CNN panel. The story was everything. Over the years, I've chased after a few that put me directly in the path of danger. It's never stopped me. The truth is a beacon. It calls me night and day, and I run after it until all the strength has left my legs and my lungs are devoid of air. It's who I am. It's how I'm built.

Seven months ago, a fire destroyed a small garage in Duburk and its chief mechanic, one Arthur McLowry, nearly died trying to free his employee, Sahir Ustad, from beneath a Buick Encore that had snagged his coveralls. McLowry freed Ustad, but then collapsed from smoke inhalation after sending his employee running for the exit. The Duburk fire brigade—an all-volunteer outfit filled with inexperienced day jobbers—did their level best to battle the blaze and get to McLowry, but the smoke was thick and black from the burning tires, and those young men were too mindful of their wives and their babies to risk the unknown.

Sahir Ustad, screaming from the street for someone to save his boss, tried to rush back into darkness himself. The police, who had gathered to block off the two-lane street, pulled him away, kicking and screaming. When I interviewed him a few days later, Ustad said he had truly believed his boss would perish in those flames. No one would risk the toxic cloud or the intense heat. He said that "in the heart of his heart" he was already in mourning.

But then, something peculiar happened—the moment that started my journey to this discovery. From the side of the blazing garage, a half-dead Arthur McLowry limped into view. He was as black as a raisin, covered in particulates and ash, but he was alive. The local ABC affiliate interviewed McLowry the next day from his room at St. Thomas and he claimed not to remember the events of the fire after freeing his employee from the grip of a determined Buick. He only remembered groggily coughing soot from his lungs as the stranger who had administered CPR slipped away. He never saw the man's face. I watched the interview from my usual perch in Flanaghan's, my pub of choice. I was hooked. I needed to know who rescued McLowry and why, in the age of Tik-Tok celebrities, the hero wasn't grabbing for his fifteen minutes of fame.

I visited the area and spoke with several witnesses to the fire, but none remembered seeing the stranger or his rescue of Arthur McLowry. When you've been in the game as long as I have, though, you aren't lacking for ideas. I stopped at the corner convenience store and asked if they had security cameras facing that general direction. Turns out, store security wasn't an issue, so no footage was to be found. The bicycle shop across the street proved to be a different story. They had three cameras, but only one of them gave me a decent angle on McLowry's garage. I slipped the manager of the shop—a hipster neckbeard named Cosmo—a couple of Jacksons, and he booted up the footage I needed. The resolution was low, and the footage lacked color, but as we watched the fire blaze, we spotted a man running behind the garage and, a few minutes later, slipping away and out of frame.

Despite its small town charm, most consider Duburk to be the armpit of Westfall County. Every other building along Main Street is empty, a hollow artifact of some bygone era. Crossland Avenue runs parallel to Main and is nearly as barren. McLowry's garage—inaccurately named Quick Fix, according to the enormous neon sign overlooking its charred remains—occupied a lot on Fallburg Lane, a cross street connecting Main and Crossland. The footage from the bike shop suggested our bashful hero had left the scene of the fire and headed west toward Main, which gave me no small amount of hope. At the corner of Main and Fallburg sat the New Alliance Credit Union and its walk-up ATM, which would mean cameras galore.

The bank footage procured by my editor, Pete Hallsy, produced a grainy photo of our mystery man. At that point, I sent his photo to a friend in the FBI and, while I waited on him to get back to me, ran a reverse image search on a platform so famous for its search engine that we all use their brand name as a verb. I couldn't have known, when I tapped 'enter' on my keyboard, the mystery I was about to step into. Each new answer uncovered three more questions as I fell into a rabbit hole of research. I spent roughly six weeks playing Sherlock Holmes while covering every other story my editor dropped in my lap. And once I had more questions than answers—when each new piece of the puzzle refused to form a single image—I drove to Wimberley, Duburk's easternmost and more charming neighbor, to meet with the pastor of Wimberley's First Presbyterian Church (PCA), one Anatole Renata.

I had called Renata under the pretense of writing a story on small town America and religion, specifically regarding poll numbers suggesting even the more rural parts of the United States are turning away from faith. He seemed hesitant to meet with me, but I assured him—okay, sure, I lied through my pearly whites—that he would not be on record. I told him I was only trying to gauge the temperature of the clergy and how such trends impact the day-to-day life of their churches. He agreed to meet with me during his lunch hour if I didn't mind conducting our interview in the park.

"I never meet with women in my office unless my wife can sit in," Renata had explained, "and they are all in Memphis, Tennessee this week for a women's retreat. So, if you don't mind watching an old man eat a salad, you can join me in the park and ask whatever you'd like."

Larue Park was as quaint and quiet as you would imagine. The gazebo at its center needed a fresh coat of paint, but the ment she wanted, and this…well, it doesn't seem like your kind of story at all, does it? Unless, of course, you're working on something else."

I smiled. How could I not? I had underestimated the man.

"Seems like you might have a bit of an investigative streak yourself, Reverend."

"My friends call me Tolly," he said, flaking the salmon with the tines of his plastic fork. "It's a silly derivative of my name, but I've never minded it."

"Fair enough."

I placed the file folder on the table between us, but didn't open it. I wanted to let him talk first.

"As for being an investigator," he said, "you must understand I've lived in Wimberley going on twenty years, Ms. Wheaton, and I've never been the interest of even our *local* paper, let alone a big outfit like the Herald. I'm not the sharpest pin in the cushion, but your phone call didn't pass the smell test. So, I did a little digging and discovered what an amazing journalist you are. I'm horrible with computers, but my granddaughter, Sarah, she's a genius with them. With her help, I tracked down and read quite a few of your pieces. You are, if I may be so bold, quite the revelation. Not to take anything away from St. John, of course."

"I'm curious why—Tolly was it?"

"Yes, ma'am."

"I'm curious why you didn't cancel the interview."

He picked at his salad and took another bite or two as he constructed his answer. I waited patiently. You don't do my job for long without learning to read the moment. My gut said

Renata wasn't thinking of a way to dodge my question. He was soul searching.

"I suppose," he finally said, dabbing at the corners of his mouth with a paper napkin, "that when you've lived long enough, life feels like it no longer holds many surprises."

He pushed the rest of his salad to one side and offered a kind smile.

"Are you a praying woman, Ms. Wheaton?"

"Not anymore," I admitted. "I grew up in church—Missionary Baptist, mostly—but, once I moved away from home, well, I guess I had little need of it. No offense."

"None taken. I think even the most devout among us have seasons of doubt…some lasting longer than others. But I've often found even the least religious offer a prayer now and again."

"I suppose in times of crisis, we all hope a higher power is paying attention. Why do you ask?"

"No reason, really. But I sometimes see patterns in the world—the ebbing and flowing of design and purpose—and I've learned to trust my instincts. Right now, they're telling me you felt the need to mislead me. Perhaps you thought I would deny you the interview if I knew your true purpose. Maybe I would have. Who can say, really, what a person will do at any given moment?"

I opened the file folder between us and pushed it toward him. He reached into the inner breast pocket of his sport coat and retrieved a pair of reading glasses before inspecting the photographs and newspaper articles I had collated. If the folder's contents surprised him, it didn't show. He seemed entirely unconcerned.

He closed the folder and slid it back to me. After removing his glasses and placing them back in the pocket from which he had retrieved them, he offered a kind smile.

"I'm curious, Ms. Wheaton, what you believe you've found."

"I was hoping you would tell me," I said. "I've seen a lot on this job and tackled my fair share of mysteries, but this…well, it doesn't add up."

The minister smiled at that the way a parent humors a toddler's attempt at a joke.

"Forgive me. That's always struck me as an odd expression," he explained.

"How so?"

"Math and science have their place, Ms. Wheaton," he said, digging around in his coat pockets for a moment before producing a pipe and a small pouch of tobacco. "They are, of course, *incredibly* useful tools—and a common grace for anyone willing to explore them. But life contains more mystery than mere science or mathematics can encompass. Wouldn't you agree?"

I have been around long enough to be wary of chasing a conversation down rabbit trails, but something about the good reverend put me at ease. Wherever he was going was not some attempt to avoid the subject I had laid before him, but a scenic route intended to provide the foundation upon which we would build the rest of our discussion. So, I climbed aboard his train of thought and rode on toward an eventual horizon.

"I'm a journalist," I countered. "I prefer facts. Feelings

matter, too, of course, but facts carry more weight. Math is all about the solution. When done correctly, we eventually reach the correct answer. And science—"

"Let's stop at math for now. You said you believe math to be all about the solution. That's incorrect. Math originates with the problem. It busies itself with uncovering the solution—that much is true—but without the problem, there is no need for the solution. John's two balloons and Jenny's two balloons are not a problem in need of solving until someone comes along to ask, 'How many balloons did they have all together?' The problem prompts the formula, the formula leads to the answer. It's all rather lovely and mechanical."

Let's say, though, that young John was born into a wealthy family and has grown accustomed to receiving fifteen balloons each time the carnival comes to town. And Jenny, born into a poor family, has never had balloons before. Likely, John feels quite poor of balloons and Jenny rich beyond what she has ever known. Factually and mathematically, yes, there are four balloons altogether. But the worth of those balloons has an extrinsic value beyond their minimal intrinsic worth. The factual, mathematical answer is only correct in a certain *limited* sense."

"I understand what you are saying," I bluffed, "but I'm not sure what this has to do with the questions that brought me here."

"Now, take science," Renata continued, stuffing tobacco into the chamber of his pipe. "I've not met an atheist yet who didn't bend the knee to the great monolith of science. They value it above all things, including their own experience. Science is a fine tool and a grand pursuit. I had a grandson once who studied the sciences. Did well for himself if I recall. But science cannot answer all our questions, Ms. Wheaton."

"You don't believe in science, Rev. Renata?" I asked. "I know people of faith sometimes shun—"

"Before you insult me, Ms. Wheaton, it might be best to let me get to my point."

I motioned for him to continue.

"Science is a wonderful and God-given tool, but it is *only* a tool. A stethoscope is also a useful tool. Used properly, it can detect a faulty heart, an infected lung, and many other defects. It cannot, however, detect Venus or predict the weather. A stethoscope cannot respond to a radio signal, nor encourage someone broken in spirit. Its usefulness has limitations. It is a fine instrument for the work it does, but it does not do all the work. Am I making any sense here, Ms. Wheaton?"

"I suppose," I said, reluctant to give him too much ground.

"Consider this: There are many tools given to us for experiencing and learning about creation. Science is merely one of them. But relying on it as your only method of understanding the world is like using only the red crayon to draw a portrait. You may create a fantastic image which closely resembles its subject, but you're setting aside an entire box of other vivid colors that would bring greater depth to the picture."

"Okay," I said, still mulling over his words. "Now, tell me what any of that has to do with the file I showed you."

"Everything, Ms. Wheaton. It has everything to do with it."

He took a moment to light his pipe, the ritual not unlike the more sacred rituals a man of the cloth is called upon to perform. It lent him an air of dignity and wisdom. He didn't need the loan.

"You've placed before me a mystery you desire to unravel," he said. "Through your lens of 2+2=4, you will never understand the great truth behind this mystery. Science could never reveal it to you, nor can you boil down the truth of it into some simplistic form that discipline *can* tackle. Whatever your background in faith may have been, you—and so many others—lack the imagination to see beyond the natural into what lies beyond it."

"So, tell me," I said, spreading the photos and documents from the file across the picnic table between us, "what explains this?"

"I'm curious about how you found me. I can only assume it has something to do with the Quick Fix over in Duburk."

"That fire would've claimed a life had you not intervened," I told him. "I found it strange a hero like you wouldn't at least check on the man whose life he saved."

"I didn't need to. Mr. McLowry made the news for three nights straight and seemed in good health each time they interviewed him."

"But your disappearance was a mystery, so I did some tracking. I finally got a look at you on an ATM camera. Got little of your face, but I got something better: your license plate number."

"And from there, a deep dive into madness."

"That's one way to look at it. I was planning on meeting with you even then. I assumed you were humble, which impressed me. But then I realized perhaps you were avoiding attention for reasons that were less honorable."

"Either a hero or a villain, eh?" Renata asked, cocking his left eyebrow. "Is your thinking always so binary, Ms. Wheaton?"

"Not at all, Tolly. I only want to get to the truth."

"You say so now, Ms. Wheaton. We'll see if you still stand on that ground once I've answered your questions."

"Obtaining the license plate led me to your name and work-place. I even found an excellent picture of you on your church's website," I said. "I had a buddy of mine—who will remain anonymous since his favors for me would likely end his employment—run facial recognition. The alphabet agencies had nothing on you. You weren't a criminal. That confounded me a bit, I admit it. I broadened the search to the entire internet using your photo as a reference. The first match I came across was this one."

I handed him a black-and-white photograph of a march down State Street in Chicago dated March 25, 1967. Led by Dr. Martin Luther King Jr., some 5,000 participants marched to the Coliseum, where Dr. King would address the crowd in protest of the Vietnam War.

"I remember this day," Tolly said. "Dr. King had been quiet about the war for some time—more pressing matters, you know —but he had finally taken a stand, and I marched with him. He was a charismatic fellow, that man. I didn't always see eye-to-eye with his theology, but I admired his indomitable spirit."

He handed the picture back to me.

"You wouldn't be here if this was all you found, Ms. Wheaton. Please continue. This is all a bit like *This Is Your Life*, I think. Of course, you're far too young to remember that program."

He was correct. I wouldn't get the reference until I looked it up long after the interview. I handed him another photo. A photographer working for The National Tribune took it in May 1946. It showed men from the Brotherhood of Railway Trainmen standing in solidarity. They were on strike for higher wages, a move which left thousands of travelers stranded. The strike would last only four days and end when President Truman intervened. Amid the group of a dozen or so soot-covered trainmen stood Anatole Renata. He appeared no younger, but certainly no older than he did as he perused the copy of that old photograph.

"George Malkin," Tolly said, pointing to another man in the photo, "was a friend of mine in those days. He'd eventually start his own business. A cobbler shop, if I recall. He'd learned the trade from his father. But in '46, both of us were working the lines. It was back-breaking work, but we saw a lot of the country, and I made some fine friends on those rails. When our union joined the strike, I went along. I didn't care about the money as much as the job, but I didn't want George and the fellows like him to be mistreated. The conditions weren't the best, and standing with them was the least I could do. The strike lasted only a few days before Truman stepped in and threatened to have the military run the lines. George stayed on the job for another few months before departing for dreams of greater riches."

"And you?" I asked.

"I stayed on another year and then left the country. I went overseas and didn't come back to the states for nearly 20 years."

"You say that as if it makes sense, Rev. Ren—um, Tolly. But here you sit, looking as if you haven't aged a day since this photograph was taken."

He smiled at me. It was disarming.

"I'm going to go out on a limb, Ms. Wheaton, and guess you have a photo in your file considerably older than 1946. What do you say, for both our sakes, you skip ahead to that one?"

I produced the item which had driven me to Tolly's door. A copy of a cyanotype image from Paris. It was hand-dated 'Spring, 1872' by the photographer. It showed a couple standing on the bridge over the River Seine. They were clearly in love.

As Tolly studied the cyanotype, a tear escaped his left eye and traveled along the side of his nose, only to cling to the side of his nostril. He brushed it away with the sleeve of his gray wool coat.

"Her name was Simonne," he said, his voice trembling with the memory. "She was a shaft of light into the blackness of doubt I had allowed into my soul. Simonne reminded me of God's grace and restored His hope with her love and devotion. She pulled me out of despair and became my partner…my wife."

"In 1872," I said, to make sure he understood exactly what he was admitting.

"1873, actually. April, if memory serves. Her parents were supportive, but they preferred a long engagement."

"You see why I'm having a hard time with this, right? You can't be more than, what, mid-50s?"

"You tell me," he said, puffing on his pipe. He seemed amused with himself.

"I have photos going back more than a hundred years, Tolly, and you look the same in all of them. A few pounds up, a few pounds down, but you're the same guy. Clearly, something strange is going on."

"So it would seem."

"I searched for relatives. I figured, hey, maybe he comes from a family with extraordinarily strong genes, you know? Maybe you had distant relatives who could pass for your twin. It didn't sound plausible to me, but I had to find an answer. That's when I discovered Anatole Renata has only existed—in any official capacity—for the last 40 years. There are no birth records. No family tree for me to climb. Nothing."

"So, you kept asking yourself questions," Tolly said.

"That's what we do. Journalists, I mean. We keep asking questions until we get answers. We dig and poke and prod and eventually—if our persistence outlives the subject's resistance—we come away with the truth."

"This is where you and I find our common ground," Tolly said. "We are seekers of the truth. You have your set of tools and I have mine. Our goals are similar: to understand something we did not before…to uncover a mystery hidden in the commonplace."

"You see, then, why I couldn't resist coming to you once I had seen the evidence collected in this file. I couldn't walk away from something this—"

"Ridiculous?"

"Intriguing," I corrected. "I know there's a solution to this conundrum. Something solid. Something my readers will buy, but I'll be damned if I can see it. Oh, sorry about the language."

"No apology necessary, Ms. Wheaton. Though, I'd offer a correction if you don't mind."

"Feel free."

"You said you'd be damned if you can see the solution. I think, rather, you're damned if you don't. But I suppose we won't know the will or won't of it all until I've told you what you came to hear."

"Please, Tolly, enlighten me."

Renata took a few puffs of his pipe as he considered how to craft his explanation. It was then I remembered the digital recorder in my purse and retrieved it.

"Would you mind if I record you? I should've asked before."

"Not at all. I assume such a thing is stock in trade for people in your field."

I pressed the record button and focused on Tolly's gentle eyes. He rubbed his chin for a moment and removed the pipe from his mouth.

"When I was a boy," he said, "I didn't have many friends. My family was poor, and I spent my childhood doing all I could to help put food on the table. I'd barely made it to adulthood when my father passed away. As the man of the house, I helped provide for my mother and sisters, though I admit I didn't carry that weight without an immature stumble or two. When my mother died, I was suddenly all my sisters had. They depended on me, not only to provide but to protect. We were a conquered people, you see. Enemy forces occupied our cities. It was a frightening season, but we created our own sense of normalcy and survived one day at a time. As I became more successful, we helped those around us in need. My sisters—even as youngsters —possessed the holy gift of hospitality. They were sensitive to the needs of our neighbors and did their best to intervene."

"You mentioned an occupation," I said. "Are we talking Nazi-occupied France, or—"

"I will answer all your questions, I assure you, Ms. Wheaton. I would, however, like to tell my story chronologically."

"I'm sorry for interrupting. Please, go on."

"My sisters and I had settled into our routine. We missed our parents, of course, but we were surviving well enough and even eked out a bit of joy now and again. Then, one day when I least expected it, I met the man who would become my truest friend."

"George Malkin?"

Tolly chuckled and shook his head.

"Oh, no. George came into my life much later, Ms. Wheaton. Much, much later."

"I'm sorry. Go on."

"It's hard for me to recall what I was doing when I first heard the stories."

"Stories?"

"My friend's reputation preceded him, you see. I was born a Jew, and though my people were often as maligned and mistreated in those days as they are today, I was faithful in my pursuit of Yahweh. I heard rumblings in the Temple of a young teacher whose knowledge of the Torah was beyond anything ever heard. The older men, of course, cared little for upstarts, but the young men spoke in whispers, questioning whether this teacher was a heretic or a prophet."

"I didn't care about those things, to be honest. I was far too busy keeping food on the table…and the wrong suitors away from my sisters. In the market one day, though, I met my friend. He was buying oil and salt and found himself short. He was prepared to put the oil back when my older sister offered to cover the shortage. They chatted after he thanked her. Being the man of the house, I stepped in. Even in those days, you didn't simply let some stranger speak with your sister. You interjected and sized him up."

He smiled at the memory.

"It's hard to say what inspires friendship, but ours was instantaneous. Before we left the marketplace, I had invited him for dinner. Both my sisters loved him as easily as I did. And I don't mean to say they had any romantic interest in him. I had not brought him home to play matchmaker, and they under-stood that. They also accepted, as they got to know him, that he was beyond such things. There was a loneliness about him which suited him, and a wife would only slow him down."

"Career-minded," I offered.

"Something like that," Tolly said, his eyes searching mine for something. In retrospect, I think perhaps it disappointed him that I hadn't figured him out yet.

"My friend was a rabbi. The same teacher I had heard so much about. For the life of me, I couldn't see why he was such a controversial figure. He had such a gentleness about him I couldn't imagine anyone seeing him as a threat or a heretic. His knowledge of the Torah, and the way he could teach it with such authority, was mesmerizing and inspiring."

"Before that first dinner was over, my sisters invited him to return. He tried to decline, as he had several men who traveled with him. He didn't want them to feel as if he was ditching them for a free meal. I assured him we had plenty for all of them and would be pleased to offer them our hospitality as well."

"I'm guessing your friendship didn't go over well with some of the more conservative members of your synagogue," I said.

"No one paid much attention to it, honestly. Not then, at least. My friend wasn't as well-known as he would come to be later. He traveled a lot, so his reputation differed from place to place. He and his friends were welcome guests every time they passed through, greeted with food and celebration."

"Knowing him changed us, Ms. Wheaton. He was transformative. When he spoke to us, it was as if he saw our greater selves—the men and women Yahweh had always meant for us to be—and spoke directly to them and not to the broken, messy selves we were in the moment. He spoke of God not as some distant king or emperor, but as a loving father or a husband willing to sacrifice all he held dear for his bride. From that point on, as I listened to the Torah proclaimed in the Temple, it became impossible not to see its truth and mystery through this new lens."

"Is that how a Jewish man ended up a Methodist minister?" I asked.

"I'm getting there."

As Reverend Renata spoke, I paid strict attention to his

mannerisms. Police officers with a few years under their belts will tell you they develop an instinct for the truth. Liars, even the best ones—the ones who craft deception so closely tied to the truth even *they* lose sight of what is real and what isn't—have ticks and tells which give them away. Investigative journalists develop that skill, too. We have a finely tuned "BS meter" to paraphrase my editor. I'm telling you this because it is important to note that, at no point in the entirety of Tolly's tale, did I feel like I was being tricked, lied to, or scammed. The man spoke with utter sincerity. I now believe it was because he had grown tired of his secret and needed someone else to help shoulder the burden. He hoped I would ultimately be that someone.

"My dear friend and teacher had been away for some time," Tolly continued, "when I became quite ill. The girls wanted to get word to him. They felt, because God shined so greatly upon him, his presence might bring healing and restoration to their sick brother. We had all heard the stories, of course, but had never seen such a thing for ourselves. As sick as I was, I ordered them to leave him out of it. His teachings had caused enough friction that people were calling for his arrest. They feared he was going to lead some governmental revolt. Such a thing was never his goal, of course, but you know how people can be, Ms. Wheaton. Give them a scrap of misinformation to hang their hats on and fan the flames with enough rhetoric and fear-mongering, and you can whip them into a violent frenzy easily enough. We still see the same sort of nonsense today."

"All too often," I agreed. "How long were you ill, Tolly?"

"I couldn't tell you," he replied. "I was in and out of

consciousness for most of it. My body would shake with tremors from a fever that wouldn't break."

"Your sisters didn't take you to a hospital?"

"We didn't have access to the sort of sophisticated medical help we have access to now, I'm sad to say. It was more of a 'watch, wait, and pray' situation. How long the relentless fever had me in its grip, though, I cannot say. I can only tell you that, once the situation became so grave that they could no longer find any room for hope, my sisters ignored my wishes and sent for my friend."

Once more, Tolly paused and searched my eyes.

"What are you looking for in there, Tolly?"

"Recognition, I suppose. But I think the math is getting in your way."

"The math?"

"No cell phones in those days," he continued, as if he hadn't left my question hanging in the air. "No telegrams, either. So, my sisters sent a messenger to tell the rabbi that I was knocking —insistently by that point—at death's heavy door. They told him they truly believed he could make a difference in the whole situation if he would only come running."

"And did he?"

"No, no. He was an extremely busy man and did not believe the situation to be as dire as my sisters made it seem. He would come visit later, though, once he finished his work."

"I'm sure you were glad to see him," I said.

"Not exactly," Tolly replied, taking a quick puff from his pipe. "By the time he arrived in Bethany, I'd been dead for four days."

Over the years, the men and women I have interviewed have made many incredible statements that have inspired me, frightened me to my core, filled me with laughter, and humbled me with the scope of humanity. Yet before that moment with Tolly, I had never found myself speechless. Whatever destination I had assumed his story would drive us to, I suddenly found myself in alien terrain. The look on my face must have been entirely ridiculous, yet Tolly just puffed away on his pipe and gave me a moment or two to process before he continued.

"Martha, my older sister, ran out to meet him on the road. She—"

"You…y-you're telling me that…that you're—"

"Lazarus? Yes, Ms. Wheaton."

"And your friend was?"

"Jesus the Christ. Do keep up."

He smiled at me so warmly I found myself with little to say. I didn't believe him, of course, but I was so enthralled by the madness of it all that I wanted to hear everything.

"Martha ran to meet him on the road and said she believed that if he had only been there before I died, things might have turned out differently. But she also said something that was a giant leap for her. God love her, she was always the cautious sort, you see? Martha loved Jesus, opened her home to him, and always treated him with the sort of respect any of us would have shown a rabbi. But it was our younger sister, Mary, who came to faith most readily. But, seeing him there, Martha said her spirit opened her mouth and spoke for her. She told Jesus that she believed, even in that dark moment four days after my death, God would hear him and grant whatever he might ask. If you had known Martha, Ms. Wheaton, you would understand how great a confession of faith it was for her. Her trust certainly moved my friend. From there, of course, you know the narrative presented in scripture. It's as accurate a telling of those events as I could ever repeat for you."

"Um, lapsed Baptist here," I said, raising my hand as if asking an elementary teacher to explain my homework assignment. "Can we pretend I remember very little about that story?"

As Tolly continued, I found no judgment in his kind eyes.

"Many around us believed Jesus was the Messiah foretold by the prophets. To me, he was nothing more or less than my best friend. Oh, I knew he was a holier man than any I had ever known, but I had wrongly assumed that the Son of Man would come as some conquering warrior. Someone to set us free from Roman captivity. Martha, though, for all her busybody ways, had come to the truth of it. Jesus was far more than a simple teacher. More than a man. In her grief, she laid it all out there. She confessed what she truly believed: that, though all evidence suggested I was long past the point of intervention, Jesus could still deliver. It turned out, of course, she was right. Jesus told her he, himself, was the resurrection. That he was life, and even death would submit to his authority."

He stopped for a moment and searched my eyes again.

"Go ahead, Ms. Wheaton. Ask your question."

"Do you remember what happened?"

"Not really, no. I only remember a feeling I had: the sensation of waiting. Not the bored sort one does as the DMV, mind you, but an expectant waiting. I found myself trapped in a moment filled with the sort of joyous and anxious exuberance of a young child when he first opens his eyes on Christmas morning. Wherever I was, Ms. Wheaton, it was akin to a waiting room. There were no sights to see…only the expectation of seeing my friend again."

"And then?"

"And then I heard him call out to me: 'Lazarus?'—the way any friend might say your name when they've spotted you across the room. But his voice reached across a much larger void. 'Lazarus?' he called again, and I ached to shout, 'I am here, my friend!' In all this time, I have not forgotten the sound of his voice. Ms. Wheaton, I retained no physical body at all. And yet, even in my formless state, I felt his words reaching out to me and tugging gently, the way an archaeologist might carefully remove a fossil from the earth. 'Come forth,' he said, and by God I did. My eyes opened to the cloth they had wrapped me in. I could barely move. But Jesus called, and I came. And when he asked those gathered to remove my wrappings, I saw a sight I had never seen before."

"What?" I asked, leaning so far across the picnic table that, to any onlookers, it might have seemed flirtatious.

"There were tears in his eyes," Tolly said, his voice catching at the recollection. "Not tears of joy for my return, mind you, but remnants of his sorrow—the toll of his great humility. And the price of becoming like us. Part of the triune God sent to us as a man and bearing the weight of our human frailty and suffering. That he would take upon himself such sorrow over the likes of me…well, I would never doubt him or his love again."

"If I may," I said, my mind spinning like a tilt-a-whirl, "can we…uh, what I mean to say is, can you confirm in plain English that you are saying what it sounds to me like you are saying?"

"I'm saying I am Lazarus, brother of Martha and Mary, citizen of Bethany, friend to Jesus of Nazareth," Tolly said as calmly as if he was talking about the weather. "I was sick and died, and Christ raised me from the dead."

"And you never died again? It just doesn't take?"

He laughed at that, the sort of belly laugh which becomes infectious. I uncomfortably chuckled along, although I felt that one—if not both—of us had lost their mind.

"I only died once," he said once his laughter subsided. "To be perfectly frank, Ms. Wheaton, I'm not sure *why* I never died again. I've developed a theory or two, of course, but I suppose I won't know for certain until my friend and I reunite at the end of things."

"What sort of theories?"

"The most interesting one—at least to me—is that my friend scared Death away from me," he replied. "She had a tight grip on me before he intervened. You can imagine how unsettling it must have been for her. Death's power seemed invincible until someone with greater authority stepped in. Perhaps she simply doesn't want to risk a confrontation. After all, Ms. Wheaton, Death knows how her story ends. Thanks to Calvary, she will be vanquished and rendered powerless. Perhaps, to her, I'm a grim reminder of her fate."

I needed to think. To process. I gathered all the photos and news clippings I'd presented and stuffed them back into the folder. Tolly remained silent, watching me with a keen eye and puffing thoughtfully on his pipe like Gandalf the Grey amused by a bumbling hobbit.

"You don't believe me," he said.

"I'm not sure what I believe. The story I came here to uncover was already...well, I don't even have a word for it. Not impossible. At least, I didn't think so. I assumed there was an answer I couldn't see."

"Surely you didn't see *this* coming," he said, wearing a hint of a smirk.

"I met a young man a few years ago," I said, smiling at the memory of an old friend. "His name was Dylan. He helped me break a big story and saved my life from the criminal cock-roaches my investigation was exposing. He was unlike anyone I've ever met...until now. You remind me of him, Tolly. There's something otherworldly about you both. Dylan didn't stick around long but, like you, he thought my eyes were closed tight to the unexplained wonders of the world. I never believed it was true, but—"

"I am confronting you with the miraculous and you aren't sure how to make it fit into the framework you've built for your-self. Either I'm a liar, a lunatic, or I'm telling you the truth. Your worldview leaves no room for my story to be true, yet your instincts argue against me being a pathological liar or having some sort of mental illness. You trust your gut and your frame-work...but suddenly must contend with something that puts them at odds. Am I close?"

I nodded, distracted momentarily by a large tow truck driving past the park entrance pulling behind it another tow truck. Not something one sees often. The scent of pipe tobacco drew me back to the reverend's eyes and his words.

"I don't think you're a liar," I said. "Crazy? I'm not qualified to make *that* kind of diagnosis."

"Fair enough."

"I believe *you* believe what you're telling me. Furthermore, I believe there's something strange going on with you, Tolly. Something I can't seem to work out. There's a part of me that, as hard as it is to fathom, believes you're unaging. Perhaps not immortal, but demonstrably more long-lived than the oldest living people who make the local news cycles as personal interest stories. I don't know how it's possible or why you're the one with this gift, but…well, here you sit. Asking me to believe you are who you *say* you are, however, is—"

"A bridge too far?"

"Well, yes. I mean, I believe Jesus was a person. He walked the earth and taught forgiveness. I even believe the core values of his teachings are valuable to society. But you're asking me to believe he truly was what they say he was."

"What *he* said he was," Tolly corrected. "My friend doesn't let you off the hook so easily. He said he was the Son of Man, a term we Jews reserved for the long-awaited messiah. We didn't lift him up as some false deity, Ms. Wheaton. We only proclaimed what we saw and heard from him. And believe me, I understand your hesitation and doubt. I do. People doubted the truth of what had happened to me even then. It didn't matter how many people had witnessed the thing or that he performed signs and miracles wherever he went. It wouldn't matter today, either. Those with ears to hear and eyes to see do so. Those waiting for the numbers to add up or the science to confirm, do not. He lived those things in front of them, and some still didn't believe. Why would *you* all these years later? No, no. It isn't a spectacle that motivates belief and devotion. It's God himself who motivates it…gives us a touch of faith enough for small, great things."

"You are asking a lot of me, Tolly," I said, shoving the file back into my bag. "I don't know what I came here hoping to find, but I'm fairly certain this wasn't it."

"You said you came here for the truth, Ms. Wheaton. If you'll recall, I said you might not stand on that ground after you heard what I had to say."

"How can I?"

"Is it so difficult? If math and science don't answer your questions, what are you left with? Math can tell you one man plus one woman plus a lifelong commitment equals a marriage. Science can tell you what falling in love does to you physiologically and what parts of your brain spring to life during sex, but where does that love come from? Why is it important? Is it merely some biological imperative and, if so, why do couples who don't want or can't have children still fall in love, marry, and have sex?"

"Ms. Wheaton, we instinctively know that there is more to life and creation around us than what we can touch, see, and understand. We lie to ourselves, of course, because we dislike having anyone else to answer to. We prefer to be our own little gods in our own insular worlds, answering to no one—our own ultimate authority. It makes it easier to cheat, divorce, swindle, and sacrifice everything at the altar of self if all that ultimately matters is what feels good and right for each of us as individuals. Our self-focus drives us further and further away from seeking deeper truths…from seeing the hand of God at work in the muck and the mess of humanity."

"What you are asking me to believe—"

"The truth?"

"—is beyond rationality," I said. "I don't have a problem with you keeping your religion, Reverend Renata. But I do not believe in miracles or the supernatural."

"You're suddenly quite formal," he replied. "And strangely *rigid* for a truth-seeker. Perhaps you aren't the one I hoped you would be."

"What does that even mean? The one what?"

"I have carried this truth for many years, Ms. Wheaton," he said, pointing at me with the lip of his pipe. "I had hoped to unburden myself to someone trustworthy. Someone for whom the truth would be sacrosanct if not sacred. It appears I ask too much of you."

I don't recall replying to that. In fact, I recall little of the rest of the day. Not the drive home. Not burning the file I had compiled on Renata. Or even the cause of the tears which woke me in the night. The next day, not fully understanding why, I drove back to Wimberley. I didn't bother calling. I found Tolly on the front steps of his church, waiting for me.

I sat next to him, not knowing what to say. The silence was deafening as I watched him fill his pipe and light it. I retrieved the digital recorder in my purse and pressed the record button.

"I wondered if I would ever see you again, Ms. Wheaton," he said at last, "or if I was a bigger fool than I previously believed. I worried my faith in you was misplaced."

"I may have been," I admitted.

"Nonsense. Your return is all the proof I need to believe it wasn't."

"For argument's sake, let's say I believe you, Tolly. If I imagine every single thing you told me yesterday was true—"

"Yes?"

"I need to know what happened after. I need to know how you got from there to here."

"You know a lot of it already," he said. "A few highlights were in your file."

"I don't mean where you went and what aliases you used, but how someone deals with being resurrected. I want to know when you first realized you wouldn't die. I need to know—"

"Yes?"

"If you have regrets."

"Hmm. I see."

Tiny puffs of smoke billowed from his pipe as if it was a cloud factory for all the Whos in Whoville.

"The witnesses didn't feel any need to keep quiet about it," he finally said. "Word of my death and resurrection spread throughout Bethany and beyond. Jesus stayed with us a short while before continuing on his way. His disciples, though they marveled at all he had done, feared the political and religious forces aligned against him would use my resurrection as some sort of proof he was a devil or something. I was sad to see my friend go, of course, but I feared his arrest. As you know, however, nothing would have prevented it."

"Did you ever see him again?"

"Yes. On the day of his crucifixion."

"You were there?"

Tolly's eyes never left mine, but his thoughts drifted far away.

"Once news of his arrest became public, I tried to find his disciples, not realizing most had scattered to the wind, fearing their own arrests. Knowing I hadn't clout or money enough to interfere with Pilate's judgement, I stood in the crowds lining the road to Golgotha, hoping to glimpse my friend, my brother. Then, through the throng of bloodthirsty onlookers, I spotted him carrying—"

Tolly did not strike me as a man who was often emotional, yet his expression suggested he needed a moment to compose himself. I said nothing.

"He was carrying his cross, though barely. He stumbled and not for the first time. The Romans compelled a man from Cyrene to carry it in his stead. Ms. Wheaton, had I not been a close friend, I might not have recognized my friend. Not even in war have seen no one beaten and bruised or beheld treatment so brutal and unjust. And, when they hung him on that torturous device which has become, for believers like me, a symbol of our hope—the sign of his finished work—I stood there among the many and watched him bleed and give up his life. The image of it still haunts my dreams now and again. How could it not?"

"And three days later?"

Tolly brushed a tear away with the back of his hand, a sudden smile breaking through his sorrow.

"Oh, I felt it even before I heard the news. His body was missing, they said. Someone had stolen it in the night. It all seemed quite mysterious to most of them, no doubt. But not to me. From the deep depths of my mourning, I felt his return stirring me to joy. It was as if all creation had been holding its breath for three days when, suddenly, it could fill its lungs again. I never got to see him, though. He appeared to his disciples, and many people saw him throughout the area over the course of the forty days which followed, but he was gone before I could get to him. If I have a regret, Ms. Wheaton, it is that."

"And when did you realize you wouldn't die?"

"It wasn't exactly an epiphany. As time passed, I watched the people around me getting older, but I never did. Martha eventually passed away and left Mary and I to mourn. Then Mary passed away and left me alone. I became all too aware of the whispers. People were asking questions and looking at me strangely…as if they hadn't done so already."

"Small town gossip," I said. "A plague not unknown to the folks here in Wimberley, I'd imagine."

"Well, aside from my congregants, folks here have never had much reason to consider me. Your newspaper article would change all that, of course, but I trust you'll do with it what you think is best."

"Once you realized your condition, for lack of a better term, what did you do?"

"I sought counsel from those who walked with him. We weren't so organized in those days, of course, and the apostles traveled in separate circles to expand the message of his life, death, and resurrection beyond the ground he had walked. They were witnesses with firsthand accounts of how he turned everything they thought they knew upside down. It was a dangerous time for all of us but, one by one, they welcomed me as a brother. Unfortunately, none of them had answers for me. If our friend had raised me with some larger plan in mind than underscoring the truth of who and what he was, he had never shared it with the likes of James and John."

"I don't know how familiar you are with the fates of the apostles, Ms. Wheaton, but things ended badly for most of them. Each served as a living sacrifice for the glory of the God they served, with some being martyred and others imprisoned. They were not the smartest men, nor the bravest, but the power of the Holy Spirit emboldened them to carry the Gospel as far and wide as they could. Upon their deaths, others took up the call, and the story of my friend and his grace spread out to the four corners of the world."

"And you?" I asked.

He turned his gaze beyond the street to the park where I had first met him the day before. The smoke from his pipe briefly clouded his soft features, but there was something in his warm, brown eyes which made it seem as if he was looking beyond the moment to an earlier time. Perhaps not remembering it so much as watching it play out like a vivid movie lighting a darkened theater.

"With the death of the last of them, I felt alone and adrift. What few remaining friends I had were old and not long for the world, so I asked one last favor of them: that they mourn me in public places and speak as though I had finally passed away."

"You faked your death?"

Tolly nodded.

"It was cowardly, but I was mourning. I felt the need to leave the world I knew behind before anyone else could leave me. So, I traveled. Once my money was gone, I begged for food. I worked for a while and was a slave several times. Over the centuries, I made fortunes and lost them. I spent seasons in solitude and years enmeshed in the lives of the people I came to know. My loneliness, however, followed everywhere I went. I journeyed throughout Asia and Ethiopia. I told no one who I really was. By that point, who would have believed me?"

"You didn't marry?"

"No. Well, not for a few centuries. Despite my great loneliness, I felt it would be awful to marry and have children, only to outlive them all. Even if I shared my secret, they would think I was mad. I also considered that my children might inherit my undying nature. What would that mean in the grand scheme of things? As wicked as a man's heart can be, what might a race of immortal men unleash upon the world? I decided it was best not to find out."

"But you're married *now*," I said. "And you married Simonne. You must have changed your mind at some point."

"Of course I did," Tolly laughed. "I am as weak a man as any you have ever met, Ms. Wheaton. Eventually, the pain of my solitude outweighed my fear of the consequences, and I stopped hiding myself from the possibility of marriage. Over the years, I have loved many families. I've raised children and grand-children. And I've watched them die."

He tapped his pipe on the step, shaking loose the smol-dering remnants of tobacco in the bowl. He placed the pipe in his pocket and took a slow, deep breath.

The day was warm though not oppressively so, and the birds in the trees were joyfully singing back and forth to one another whatever stories the birds share. A cool breeze lifted the tobacco ashes from the steps and carried them down the street like a murmuration of starlings. I watched them go and looked back to find Tolly weeping.

"There is sorrow in every passing," he said after a moment. "Sometimes, death is grace. Many times, it's expected. I've found, though, such loss always feels unfair. I've spent too many days to count weeping over my children and theirs."

"It's a cycle, you see? I love and lose then hide away. I've removed myself from being an active participant in the world many times. But, always, the seclusion prompts me to reengage. I love again, lose again, then hide again. It is endless and horrible and beautiful and sad and joyful and cruel and gracious and…it is who I am."

I took his hand in mine. To this day, I don't know why. I can't tell you I believed his story at that moment, but I believed his sorrow. I felt it radiating from him as tangibly as the kind-ness and hospitality I had felt before.

"Did you ever lose faith?" I asked.

"In Christ? No, dear. Not in him. In the purpose of me? In the plan? Of course. How could I not? I am a frail human being and just as prone to wander into self-focus as any man who has ever lived. So, yes, I had seasons of doubt. Moments when faith took a backseat to self. Dark nights when I questioned my place in it all. What if the surrounding hysteria had caught me and I had bought a ticket for the ride? What if I was a fool?"

"I hear a 'but' in there."

He pulled a handkerchief from his pocket to wipe the tears from his eyes.

"No matter how far I drifted, Ms. Wheaton, I couldn't escape the tender sound of his voice. Regardless of what name I hid myself under, I could still hear him calling, 'Lazarus!' And as I had one day so long ago in Bethany, I answered his call. I realize I might never know why. I may never understand what has happened to me or its grander purpose, but I trust him. And just as I had felt that sense of waiting after my death, the sweet expectation that I would see him again, I feel I am waiting once more. Caught in the in-between. Whether I live until his return or not, I trust I will see him again face-to-face. And that's enough for me. It took me hundreds of years to get to this point, but it's enough. With that realization, I decided that, although I had missed my chance to travel with the apostles and spread the story of the messiah to the hurting world, I could at least share it with those around me. I could be a simple minister in a small-town church. I could point men, women, and children to the truth and they, too, could be called from the grave of their day-to-day existence and into a new life."

"Why tell me all this?" I asked. I knew, of course, that I had come to him for answers, but it would have been easier for him to lie to me or try to convince me of something I would be more willing to believe. Instead, Tolly had told me the least convincing story I had ever heard with all the conviction of a small child telling you what they want for their birthday. There was a realness—for lack of a better word—to Anatole Renata that I could not deny no matter how I felt about religion and the supernatural.

"You found me out," he said, giving my hand a squeeze. "You were a Godsend, sweet girl, in that you gave me a reason to stop hiding. When I received your call the other day, I remained utterly unconvinced by your stated motivation. So, I prayed."

"For what exactly?"

"For you exactly," he chuckled. "That you would be someone I could trust. One who would hear me and not run away thinking I was a lunatic. That at long last, I could be myself without fear. Even if you don't believe me, Ms. Wheaton, you have given me a wonderful gift. I pray God will bless you a thousand-fold for your kindness to me. And since I am now free of this weight I have carried, I pray God will grant me rest. I have grown weary of this place and—"

"And you miss your friend," I finished for him.

"Yes. I long to hear his voice again without the veil between us. But, if I must tarry until his return, I will do so as his servant…assuming, of course, the publication of your story does not take that from me."

I smiled at him. I'd be lying to say a small part of me didn't worry that I was being taken for a sucker.

"I don't have any intention of sharing your story, Tolly. Whatever is or isn't true about you, I believe you're a good man. I may never have the sort of faith it would take to believe everything you've told me, but I think I have a bit of faith in *you*. That's enough for me."

"But what of the mystery, Ms. Wheaton? What of the eternal search for truth? The need for answers?"

I considered his questions for a moment and stopped my recorder.

"I got very little sleep last night, Tolly. Our conversation stayed with me and turned my brain into Swiss cheese. I came back this morning because I realized, whatever the truth may be, some things are better left a mystery. Not every question needs answering. I came back to *hear* your story, not to tell it."

"Then God has answered my prayers, and blessed me with a new friend."

"Will you stay here?" I asked him. "Or will you disappear into some new identity?"

"I plan to stay put," he said with a wink. "How else would you be able to find me when you feel like talking?"

I smiled at the suggestion, but had no intention of becoming his friend. Yet, several times a month, I sat across from him in Larue Park, eating lunch and talking about his long, strange life and my considerably shorter one. I asked questions about faith, told him more about my friend Dylan, and learned about myself through his grace and wisdom. I was driving home one afternoon from one of our many lunches when I realized he had indeed become a friend and confidant. And the closest thing I had to a pastor.

Eleven months later, when I received a call from his wife, Helen, I dropped everything and drove to Wimberley to meet her at the small community hospital which seemed, at least to my eyes, not to have upgraded their facilities since the mid-1970s. She explained Tolly had collapsed on the steps of his church, clutching his chest. She and one of the church deacons had rushed him to the hospital immediately, but the damage to his heart was catastrophic. They had kept him alive, but so far as they could tell, they had only briefly forestalled the inevitable.

"Tolly asked for you," Helen said as she embraced me. "You've become such a dear friend, Nevaeh—a daughter not of blood, but of choice. I've tried to encourage him and keep him fighting, but I think he knows time is short."

I walked back to Tolly's room to find him attached to thoroughly modern equipment, despite their outdated surroundings. I was no doctor, but I had been around long enough to understand some readings. It wasn't good. His eyes were closed but, when I gently took his hand, they fluttered open and focused on me. It likely took what little strength he had left to muster a smile, but he did. And I wept.

"Save those sweet tears, my young friend," he said, his voice ragged and weak. "This day is a prayer answered."

I shook my head defiantly. I had never felt so powerless.

"I don't want you to go," I whispered, mentally chiding myself for my selfishness.

"I know. But you, my child, have given me such a lovely gift. You *listened*…and gave me a chance to be myself again. For you to have taken my secret upon yourself was grace to me. I have been thankful for you, Neveah, since the moment we met."

I kissed his forehead, baptizing it with my tears.

"When you see your friend again, Lazarus, put in a good word for me?"

He smiled at me weakly.

"I will."

Helen came back to the room, and we stood there on each side of him, holding one of Tolly's hands. His children and grandchildren were inbound from other parts of the country, but wouldn't quite make it on time.

On a peaceful autumn day, my friend, Rev. Anatole Renata, finally left this hard earth behind.

I wept for him…as Jesus had so many years before.

# ACKNOWLEDGMENTS

- Heidi, my wife, my partner, my friend. I couldn't do what I do without your input and encouragement.
- B., Ember, and Jacob, for loving your old man. I couldn't be more proud to be your dad.
- Hope Coffee Co. (Sellersburg, IN) and the Mains family, for the coffee, the fellowship, the friendship, and letting this weary writer take up space while I'm working on whatever is next.
- Northside Christian Church (New Albany, IN) for giving me a spiritual home, sharpening my faith, and building a community I'm proud to be part of.

# ABOUT THE AUTHOR

*photo by Shawn Crone*

J. Patrick Lemarr lives in Indiana with his wife, Heidi, and their children. When he isn't crafting horror and fantasy, he is writing exclusive content for his Patreon supporters. Learn more at www.jpatricklemarr.com.

patreon.com/jpatricklemarr

amazon.com/author/jpatricklemarr

goodreads.com/jpatricklemarr

facebook.com/theofficialjpatricklemarr

x.com/jpatricklemarr

instagram.com/jpatricklemarr

threads.net/@jpatricklemarr

ALSO BY J PATRICK LEMARR

Shadow Plays

All That Waits in the Night

The Christmas Cabin

The Willing, The Wounded, and The Wizard

Milton Keynes UK
Ingram Content Group UK Ltd.
UKHW021901231024
450133UK00016B/1099